THE PROTECTORS

FRANK VICTORIA

THE PROTECTORS
by Frank Victoria

Published by

CityScapePress.com

Book design by Nick Zelinger, NZGraphic.com
Book Consultant-Judith Briles, TheBookShepherd.com

ISBN: 979-8-9883832-3-9 (paper)
ISBN: 979-8-9883832-4-6 (ebook)

LCCN: 2023918650

First Edition

Printed in the United States of America

PROLOGUE

A woman walked down a dimly lit city street, her heels clicking on the sidewalk. It's late and there are no other pedestrians in sight. She stopped and lit a cigarette, inhaled deeply, then exhaled and continued walking.

A half block in front of her, a man hid in an alley, his back pressed against a wall. He peeked around the corner, watched her approach, then snapped back out of sight. As the woman neared they alley, the man stiffened and prepared to snatch her.

A few blocks away another man walked. He stopped. His eyes darted from side to side. His nose twitched as he sniffed the air. Then, he bolted to the alley and arrived just as the man waiting for the woman grabbed her, put his hand over her mouth, threw her to the ground and ripped open her blouse. The other man leapt at the attacker—transformed in mid-air into a wolf—and tore out the criminal's throat.

The woman's eyes bulged with fear, but the wolf slowly backed away with its tail and head lowered, turned and ran away.

CHAPTER ONE

Troy Wellstone listened to the TV news as he prepared breakfast. He's a handsome man in his early thirties, tall and thin, but well-muscled. His thick dark brown hair is combed straight back. He moved in a graceful, almost feline manner. From the TV, he heard a reporter say, "A criminal was killed by what the intended victim said was a large dog or wolf."

Troy spun toward the TV and saw the reporter standing in an alley, "The incident occurred here last night," the reporter said. "The woman was pulled into this alley and knocked down when the animal appeared and killed her assailment."

Troy shut the TV, grabbed his phone and dialed. It's answered on the first ring.

"Did you hear the news?" he asked.

"Yes," a male voice answered. "I was just about to call you."

"It sounds like another one," Troy said. "Be sure everyone stays alert for it. We'll meet at the cabin as soon as we find out more."

* * * * *

A wolf strode through streets and alleys sniffing as if looking for food, occasionally stopping to urinate on a telephone pole or fence. It intermittently scratched on a tree.

His head and ears perked up. In the distance, someone shouted.

"Help! Someone help! Call the police!"

The wolf raced to the sound and saw two men struggling on the second floor porch of a three story building. One knocked the other down, drew a pistol and pointed it at the victim.

"No!" the victim pleaded. "Don't shoot! You've got the money. There's no point in killing me."

As the wolf raced toward the men, it saw another wolf leap from the ground to the porch. It bit into the hand holding the gun, then ripped out the gunman's throat. It stepped back, jumped to the ground and ran off.

The first wolf followed, barking as it ran. The other wolf stopped and turned to face it. Its ears were pulled back and its teeth bared, its snout still soaked with blood. It growled. The first wolf slowed and dropped its head submissively. The two wolves approached each other cautiously and sniffed one another from head to tail. Then, they each step back.

The first wolf transformed into a human being.

It's Troy.

"Don't be afraid," Troy said. "I know what you are because I'm just like you. There are others like us. You're welcome to join us. We've been looking for you for a month."

The other wolf hesitated, but also took human form. He's five foot, ten inches tall with a stocky build.

"Who has?" the other man asked.

"All of us," Troy answered. "The whole pack. We want to help. That's why we tried to find you."

"I thought so. I've noticed your scent and markings. I wanted to look for you, but I was ... I was afraid. I didn't know what to expect."

"I understand. We were all like that until we found each other."

The other man shook his head, then rubbed his temples. "What am I? I was an ordinary person. What happened? How did I become a wolf? Why am I killing people? What ..."

Troy held up his hands. "Wait. We'll explain everything to you. For now, just know that you've done nothing wrong and that there are others like you. You'll be among friends."

The other man sighed. "Okay. That sounds good. Now what?"

Troy smiled. "There's a parking lot two blocks north of here. I'll pick you up there tomorrow morning at ten and we'll go meet the rest of the pack."

The other man nodded. "Okay. Thank you. Thank you very much."

Troy stepped to him. "You're going to be fine. What's your name?

"Kevin. Kevin Colson. Yours?"

"Troy Wellstone."

Troy holds out his hand and Kevin shakes it.

CHAPTER TWO

Troy drove down a dirt-and-gravel forest road with Kevin in the passenger seat.

"This will take us to our cabin where you'll meet the others," Troy told Kevin.

"I'm looking forward to it."

"You won't be disappointed."

"Why does this happen at a later age?" Kevin asked.

"It varies. Anywhere from twenty-one to thirty. We don't know why."

"It's a shame," Kevin said, "I had a good job. I was a salesman, sold computer equipment. Made good money. But I couldn't function. I couldn't concentrate on what I was doing. I had a lot of time on my hands, and started drinking—a lot. I think I may be an alcoholic. I can't get past a day without booze."

"We'll help. Others in the pack have had problems like that."

"Really?"

"Yep. Tom was a drinker, too. Now, he's clean and sober. Still goes to AA meetings."

"No kidding?"

"Yeah, and Miriam was hooked on heroin. She became a call girl to support her habit. We got her help and now she's fine."

"Well, how did …"

"Let's hold off on the questions until we're with the pack. You'll find out everything."

* * * * *

Troy pulled up near the door of a large log-and-stone cabin. Three other cars were parked in the same area. When he got out of the car and walked to the door, it opened and he was greeted by Julia Mitchell, a comely redhead.

"Welcome, Kevin. I'm Julia."

She hugged him, then gestured them forward. "Please come in. Everyone is eager to meet you Kevin."

She led them into a spacious living room where two men and another woman stood to welcome them.

"John should be here any minute," Julia told Troy. "Miriam and Hannah are coming together. They won't be long."

She stood aside and Troy introduced Kevin to Diana Lake, a beautiful brunette. She held out her hand to Kevin, then leaned over and kissed him on the cheek.

"Welcome Kevin. I'm so pleased to meet you." A tall, thin man extended his hand. "I'm Tom Blake. It's good to have you here."

Kevin shook Tom's hand. "It's good to be here."

A man behind Tom stepped forward. "My name is Barry Goldman." He threw his arm around Kevin and hugged him. "Welcome to the pack."

"Thank you," Kevin said.

They heard car doors slam shut.

"That must be the others," Julia said. She walked to the door and opened it to two lovely women and a stately gentleman in a business suit. One of the women smiled in anticipation. "Is he here yet?"

Julia nodded. "He sure is. Just got here."

They walked into the living room. Hannah Dale, a slender but shapely woman with long blonde hair, approached Kevin first and shook his hand. "I'm very happy to meet you."

She gave him a hug.

Kevin smiled. "It's my pleasure."

The man, in his early thirties, grabbed Kevin's hand and squeezed it tightly. "I'm John Sacks. It's a pleasure to have you here. You're among your own kind. And I'll bet you're thrilled."

"I am. I certainly am."

"How long were you out there not knowing what you were."

"About five months."

The last woman, a striking strawberry-blonde with her hair in a ponytail approached Kevin with a broad smile and a hug. "Welcome, Kevin. I'm Miriam Hill. Welcome aboard."

Troy smiled at Kevin. "Bet you feel better already."

Kevin grinned. "I do. I feel like I'm with family."

"You are," Julia said.

Troy sat and the others did the same.

"Well," Troy said. "let's get Kevin up to speed on who and what we are. Where do we start? Carlo?"

"Yeah. Right from the beginning," Tom said.

Troy pursed his lips. "Carlo Maggio was a doctor and a brilliant biologist. One of his discoveries made him wealthy, and he opened his own laboratory to work independently. He died not long ago. But about four years earlier, he was attacked by two muggers."

"They stole his wallet and wristwatch," Tom said. "They knocked him to the ground and started kicking him. They might have killed him, but a wolf arrived and killed one the muggers. The other one pulled a gun and shot the wolf, who still managed to kill the gunman. Then, the wolf went unconscious and changed into human form. That happens when we lose consciousness. We automatically revert to our human form. Same when we die."

"That wolf," Miriam said, "was Troy."

Kevin whipped his head toward Troy. "Wow! Then what happened?"

"When I regained consciousness, Carlo was kneeling over me checking my wound. He asked if I could walk, so I struggled to my feet. He held on to me and we staggered to his car, which was close by. When I got inside, I passed out again and don't remember anything until I woke up in bed the next morning. My wound was bandaged and Carlos was sitting next to me.

"He said that the bullet hadn't severed any major arteries and that he'd fixed it fairly quickly and easily. But he wasn't through with me. He drew a number of blood samples and questioned me about myself, you know, my age, background, health history, when did I first transform in a wolf. I was free to come and go as I pleased, but for the next five days, I was there every day for him to check my wound.

"About three weeks after I was shot, Carlo and I had dinner at his place and he explained what was going on. I had a rare and unique gene that compelled me to use my powers to protect ordinary humans. He didn't know why, and we still don't know why that is."

"A gene?" Kevin asked.

"Right. I don't know how he figured it out. He explained it once, but it was way over our heads." Kevin looked bewildered. "So, this is inherited."

"Exactly."

Kevin thought for a moment. "Well, how did you find each other?"

"Troy figured there might be more like him," John said. "So, when he patrolled, he left his scent and markings and tried to pick up a trace of another one. He finally found Barry."

"What a wonderful experience." Barry said. "A revelation. I was at my wits end, on the verge of suicide."

Yeah," Kevin said. "I thought of that too."

"I think we all did at one time or another," Diana said.

The others nod in agreement.

"Anyway," Barry continued, "Troy and I looked for others. I found John and he found Tom and Diane, and so forth. "

"I see," Kevin said. "But how do you get by? I couldn't."

"Neither could we," Troy said, "until we formed the pack. Tom and I are both writers and Diana is a commercial artist. We pooled our money and started a trade magazine, which was very successful. We trained Barry and Miriam and we all work at the magazine. John has his own law practice, and Julia runs a mail order business. Hannah is a private duty nurse and an emergency medical technician. That makes us available whenever we're needed. We don't answer to anyone who's not one of us."

"Yeah, well, I've got to do something," Kevin said. "My savings are almost gone."

"You were a salesman?" Troy asked.

"Yes. I sold computer software."

"We're starting a new magazine next month. We'll need another advertising salesman. We'll train you. You can make a good buck."

"Thank you. That sounds fine."

"Any questions?" Troy asked Kevin.

"Yes. Besides Troy, have any others been wounded or killed?"

"Four have been killed," Julia said. "Two by the criminals they attacked and two by the evil ones."

Kevin's eyes narrowed. "Evil ones?"

"Right," Troy said. "They're the werewolves of lore, who feast on human flesh and blood. They don't have the gene we do."

Kevin raised his hands. "Wait. Wait. Werewolves don't die. They're eternal unless they're shot with a silver bullet by someone who loves them."

Troy snickered and shook his head. "Mythology. Our senses in human form are almost as keen as when we're in wolf form. We can endure more pain than ordinary humans, we heal faster, and we're stronger and faster. But we can be hurt. We can be killed."

"How do you know about the evil ones?" Kevin asked.

"We run into each other from time to time," Troy explained, "and it gets savage. We don't care for their habits, and they don't care for ours."

"How many are there?" Kevin asked.

"Don't know for sure," Troy answered, "but from the size of their territory we figure about twenty-five or thirty."

"Wow," Kevin said. "Then we're badly outnumbered."

"Yes. But they're only in wolf form during a full moon, and it takes them a minute or so to transform. They have no control over it. We can change into wolves and back to humans whenever we like in a moment. Anything else?"

He glanced at each of them. "Just one more. I don't want to offend anyone but … well, isn't what we do illegal, maybe immoral? I mean, we're judge, jury, and executioner."

"We've discussed that," John answered. "But the people we kill are in the act of their crime when we strike. And we only kill when a life may be in danger."

Silence for a few moments. Then Troy asked, "Are you with us?"

Kevin hesitated for a moment, then. "Yes. Gladly."

CHAPTER THREE

Kevin rode with Troy through a nearby suburb. "You'll patrol with me until you learn the ropes," Troy said. "Then you'll go it alone in a specific territory."

"Fine."

"You'll have this suburb. It's not very big and there's not much crime."

"Is that permanent?"

"No. All of us have to know various territories. I'll familiarize you with this one today."

"Sounds good. By the way, how do you tell each other apart when you're in wolf form?

"By scent. Plus, all the evil ones are dark colored. Our pack is light colored—gray, light brown, auburn. Julia really stands out. Her paws are white. Sometimes we kid her and call her white slippers. Anything else?"

"Yeah. There's one thing that I thought was too personal to bring up in front of the whole pack."

"Go ahead."

"Are any of you married? Or do you have boy-friends or girlfriends?"

"We try to avoid serious, long-term relationships."

"How come?"

"What if there's a baby? Would it be an ordinary human being or a werewolf? And if it's a werewolf, would it be like us or the evil ones?"

"What about a vasectomy or tubal ligation?"

"We've tried. It doesn't work. We regenerate. In a month, we're back to what we were. That's why we're supposed to keep involvements short and sweet. It's not carved in stone. But it's an unwritten rule."

Troy sighed and looked away. "But I've broken it."

"No kidding. When?"

"Julia and I. About three years ago. But I broke it off. We were taking too big a chance. She was hurt badly. She actually left the pack for a several months to pull herself together."

"What about with ordinary humans?"

"Same thing."

Troy nibbled his lower lip and looked as if he's making a confession. "But I did that, too. About a year ago."

Troy looked embarrassed. "It's one of my failings, Kev. A character flaw. "

"No one gets everything right.

"Nah. I'm the pack leader and should set an example. Looking back, though, it seems as if it were inevitable."

"Just happened, huh?"

"Yeah. Something clicked. It was like I had no control over it."

"How long did it last?"

"I ended it after about nine months. It broke our hearts, but we had to live with it."

CHAPTER FOUR

Troy sat with pack members at a conference table in his office. He had a stack of papers four inches thick in front of him. He put a hand on it.

"Well, we've had a week for each of us to go through this. Carlo wouldn't have left us these notes in his will if they weren't important."

"I couldn't make much out them," John said.

"It looks like they may have something to do with genetics," Hannah said.

"Yeah. That's possible," Miriam chimed in." Didn't Carlo say he was trying to develop a serum to cure Lycanthropy?

"Lycanthropy?" Kevin asked. "What's that?"

Hannah turned to Kevin. "Lycanthropy is the scientific term for werewolfism."

"Yes," Tom said. "Carlo said something about that, but we don't have the backgrounds to know if that's what these notes are about. Hannah's a nurse and all she can say is that they might involve genetics. In short, we're stumped. We may never find out."

Barry looked at Troy. "There's one thing we might try, if Troy is willing."

"I've been thinking about it," Troy responded. "But I haven't seen her in almost a year.

"Who's that?" Kevin asked.

"Two years ago," Tom said. "Troy saved a woman named Barbara Lane."

"That's the woman I told you about the other day," Troy noted.

"He didn't do it as a wolf," Tom continued. "He was in human form and saw two guys trying to pull her into their van. He beat the two guys senseless and called the police. Then, he took Barbara to the emergency room to be sure she was all right. They started seeing each other and … well, I think you understand."

Troy sighed. "She was beautiful, brilliant, witty. I've never been so attracted to anyone. We fell in love, but, as I told you, I ended the relationship."

Kevin looked puzzled. "What's that got to do with the notes?"

"She a microbiologist," Troy said. "Does a lot of research on genetics."

Kevin's eyes widened. "She might be able to interpret the notes."

"Correct. But I'm reluctant to contact her. I'm afraid we'd pick up where we left off."

"Couldn't you control your emotions?" Miriam asked.

"I don't know. I'm really drawn to her."

"It's worth a try."

The others gesture their agreement.

Julia stood. "Well, I don't. If he doesn't want to see her, that's it. Why are you all badgering him?"

"It could help us, that's why," Tom said. "Maybe it's a cure. Who knows? It's worth a shot at getting a normal life."

Julia shook her head. "I still think you're wrong to push him. He wasn't the same for months after he broke up with her."

Tom stared at Julia. "Why are you so upset about this?"

"I'm not upset. I just don't think we should force him to do something he doesn't want to."

"It's okay, Julia," Troy said. "Tom's right. It could help us. All right, I'll call her tonight."

*　*　*　*　*

Troy sat at an upscale restaurant bar sipping a brandy, awaiting Barbara. The notes were in a briefcase on the floor next to him. He'd ordered a glass wine for her.

Barbara Lane appeared shortly, and she's ravishing—long blond hair, wide blue eyes and a traffic-stopper figure. He stood, they greeted each other, and she sat on the barstool next to him.

Troy looked her over. "I don't think I have to tell you how beautiful you look."

"Thank you," Barbara answered. "You're looking very well yourself. How have you been?"

"Fine. Nothing to complain about. I'm feeling good, and the magazine is doing well."

Barbara noticed the wine. "Ah. What a nice surprise." She took a sip, looked up and rolled her eyes in delight. "Ruffino Chianti. One of my favorites. You remembered."

"Some things are hard to forget. How have you been?"

"Well, I'm over you at least. I'm just fine and I still love my work."

They were silent for a few moments. Then, Barbara said, "I have to admit you nearly knocked me over when you called. You said you needed help with something."

"Yes, I do. But it's complicated, Barb, and I'd like you not to pry too deeply into it.

Barbara gave him a suspicious look. "Why not?"

"It's important, Barb. Very important."

She hesitated and took another sip of wine. "Okay. Tell me what it's about."

Troy reached into his briefcase, took out the notes and placed them on the bar in front of her. "I need you to look over these notes and tell what the guy who wrote them was up to. I think it has to do with genetics, so it's in line with your expertise."

She leafed through the notes. "You're right that it relates to genetics. But I'd have to study them thoroughly to find out what they're about."

"Take your time. And thank you. I appreciate this."

"No need for that. I'm doing a friend a favor, that's all."

"All right. We'll keep it at that."

"Now, how about that dinner I promised you?"

CHAPTER FIVE

Troy and Tom sat across from each other at Troy's desk.

"So, what's up?" Tom asked.

"I know it's short notice, but I'd like you to take my place at the publisher's conference tomorrow. I was going to leave at four this afternoon. Can you make it?"

"Sure. But what's going on?"

"Barbara called me. Says she's got to see me right away."

"About the Carlo's notes?"

"Yes. But she wouldn't give me any details. It sounded urgent."

* * * * *

Barbara sat next to Troy on a sofa in her living room with the notes on her lap.

"Sorry to have you come over," she said. "But this is crucial if I'm going any further on this project. "

She tapped the notes.

"Why? Can't you figure out what he was doing?"

"Oh, I know what he was trying to do all right. That's why you're here."

"Okay. Let's have it."

"He was trying to manipulate the genetic structure of one kind of gene into another kind. What's interesting is that he wasn't working on guinea pigs or lab rats."

"Really. What then?"

"It's on subjects that seem to have both human and animal genes. He apparently wanted to create a serum to eliminate the animal DNA and make it completely human."

"Can you do that?"

"Yes, I can. But I won't until I know what this is about."

"What do you need to know?"

"I have to know the purpose, know how it's going to be used."

"Can't you make an exception?"

Barbara shook her head. "Absolutely not. And you're out of line in asking me to. I won't do it unless I know how it's applied. It's dangerous and unethical."

Troy stood and paced. He started to speak, then stopped. He looked at her. "Barb, this is very important."

"Tell me why."

Troy sat back down and took a deep breath. "All right. If that's the only way. It's going to be hard to believe. But you've got to."

Barbara crossed her arms and stared at him.

"Have you heard about wolves protecting people?" Troy asked.

"Yes. But those were terrified people. They can hallucinate."

"So, you don't believe in werewolves."

"In someone's imagination maybe. But that's about it."

"No, Barb, they do exist, and I can prove it."

"How?"

"I'm … I'm one of them. A werewolf."

"What's this about, Troy? Why are you doing this? Werewolf. Cut it out."

"Barb, please listen. I'll show you if you want."

"Show me what? There's no way …"

"Yes, there is. I'm going to transform. Now, control yourself. This is going to be scary. But don't panic. I'd never hurt you."

"There better be a punchline coming, Troy. This is getting out of hand. I'm a scientist, not a fool."

"Then, you'll have to believe your own eyes. You'll see for yourself. Remember, stay calm."

Barbara's eyes bulge and she puts her hand over her mouth as Troy transformed. She gasped.

Troy approached her slowly, submissively.

Barbara sucked in her breath. "Oh my god!"

She jumped up and backed away from him. Troy stepped back, then slowly toward her again. Barbara stiffened and looked away. Troy brushed past her, then turned and licked her hand.

She screamed. "No! No, don't … don't touch me! Stay away."

Barbara stared at him, eyes still protruding. She collapsed on the couch. Troy went to human form and stepped to her. He ran his fingers through her hair. Barbara's eyes fluttered, then opened. She saw Troy and turned away. Troy caressed her face, but she pushed him away and Troy stood back.

"I'm sorry. Can I do anything?"

Barbara shook her head. "No. Just let me catch my breath and calm down."

"Okay. Can I get you something? Water? Some wine or a brandy?"

She pushed herself up to sit. She took a deep breath and rubbed her temples.

"Do you want me to leave?"

"Maybe … I mean … no, no. I'll be all right. Just give me a few minutes to relax."

Barbara's eyes fixed on Troy as if he were a cobra ready to strike. They sat silently for a few moments.

"I'm sorry. But I had to show you or you'd never have believed me."

"Good lord. I'm still not sure I believe it. I don't want to."

"Try to calm yourself. You're in no danger. You know that, don't you?"

Barbara nodded. "Yes. Yes, I do."

"Feeling any better?"

"A little. But I'm trembling."

"You're still stunned."

Barbara lowered her head and rubbed the back of her neck, then looked up at Troy.

"How did it happen? Were you bitten by a were-wolf?"

"Not that I know of. And I think I'd remember that. It just happened about eight years ago."

"Are you …?"

"Yes. I'm one who helps people."

"Why? What makes you do it?"

"Sit back and I'll tell you all about it."

CHAPTER SIX

Troy walked down a dark street and heard a man shouting. He streaked toward the sound and saw three me beating a man in a commuter train station parking lot. He ran toward them, changed to wolf form. He attacked one of the muggers and killed him instantly, then went after another. The third ran away and, after killing the second mugger, Troy chased the one trying to escape.

A police siren wailed, and the lights atop the squad car swirled. It stopped and two policemen got out and fired at Troy, but missed. The intended victim stood and shouted, "No! Don't shoot! It saved me."

The policemen looked at each other quizzically and holstered their weapons.

* * * * *

Watch Commander Alan Sloan, heavy set with a partially bald head, looked at two police officers.

"This is quite a report. You say a big dog or wolf attacked three men who were mugging someone. It killed two and was chasing a third when you shot at it."

"That's correct, sir," one of the officers said.

"But the victim yelled at you to stop because the dog, or wolf, or whatever, had saved him."

The other policeman nodded. "That's right. We both saw it."

"This isn't the first time, but we've never had officers at the scene. Odd, but it seems to only kill bad guys. I'll see what the Commissioner wants to do."

He dismissed the officers and called Police Commissioner Ken Thatcher, husky with a dark complexion and thick brown eyebrows.

"We've got another one of those canine-kills-criminal occurrences."

"When?"

"Last night. Three guys were beating a man when the animal showed up."

"Yeah. Well, this has got to stop. But we can't start shooting dogs and wolves willy-nilly all over the place."

Thatcher paused and drummed his fingers. "There is something we could try."

"What's that?"

"We set up decoy incidents, stage muggings or rapes. If the animal shows, we hit it with a tranquilizer and have it examined."

"Maybe. But I wonder if we should. It's not hurting anyone but criminals. Why don't we just leave it alone?"

"What! Forget it! I'm surprised you'd say that. I don't care if it kills criminals. It kills people. Period! And I won't have it. Understood?"

"Understood. But I don't get your outburst."
"Well, you hit a nerve. You're a sworn peace officer, dammit! How can you justify what you said? Don't suggest that again. Clear?"

"Crystal."

* * * * *

Troy sat on a bench in Lincoln Park awaiting Barbara. He stood as she approached. They sat on the bench and Troy looks at her. "What's wrong? You look troubled."

"Was it one of yours last night? On the news they said police shot at a wolf who rescued someone."

"Yes. As a matter of fact, it was me."

"Does that happen a lot?"

"No. The police usually show up after everything's over."

"That bothers me." "Don't let it. We can't just stop."

He tilted his head, looking curious. "Is that all that's on your mind?"

Barbara leaned her head back and sighed. "No. I'm torn, Troy. I want to get that serum, but I don't know if I want to because of my feelings for … the feelings I had for you or because it's right to do."

"Don't let your feelings interfere. What if we can inoculate the evil wolves? We'd save lives they'd otherwise take."

Barbara stood and stepped away. She rubbed her temples, thinking. Troy said nothing. She went back to the bench.

"Okay. I'll do it. Maybe I'm right, maybe I'm wrong. But I'll do it."

"Thank you, Barb. Thank you very much."

He stood and took one of her hands. Barbara turned her head away. There were tears in her eyes, but she wouldn't let Troy see them.

"I really have to go. I'll call if anything develops."

CHAPTER SEVEN

Troy was on patrol and heard screams coming from a nearby gangway. He took wolf form and sped to the site, where two men were assaulting a woman. As he neared them, another man appeared with a rifle, and the woman and the muggers turned toward him. Troy slowed, then started to run away, but the police hit him with a tranquilizer dart. He struggled, but finally succumbed to the drug and fell. The police approached as Troy changed into a human.

One of the policeman stared at Troy. "Holy shit! What happened? Was he wearing a disguise?"

"That was no disguise," the policewoman said.

"A werewolf? That can't be".

"We all saw it," said the third policeman. "What else could it be?"

"Who's going to write the fucking report on this?" said the fourth officer. "Let's cuff him and get him to the station."

* * * * *

Troy, handcuffed, was led by two policemen into Watch Commander Sloan's office. They sit him in a chair across Sloan's desk, then stand by the door.

"I'm Watch Commander Alan Sloan. How are you?"

"I'm groggy," Troy said. "but I feel all right. Why am I in jail?"

"We'll get to that, but you'll have to answer some questions first."

"I won't say anything. I want to know my rights. I want to call a lawyer."

"I don't think I have to Mirandize a wolf."

"Do I look like a wolf?

"Not now, but according to four cops you were a wolf."

"I'm not saying anything until I talk to my lawyer."

Sloan acquiesced. He has one of the policemen uncuff Troy and gives Troy the phone. Troy dials John Sacks.

"John, it's me, Troy. I've been arrested. Can you bail me out?"   "

Are you all right?"

"I'm fine."

"I'll be there in forty minutes."

Troy returned the phone.

"Your identification says you're Troy Wellstone. Is that right?"

"Yes."

"And what do you do?"

"I'm a magazine publisher. And that's all I'll say without a lawyer."

Sloan looks at the two officers. "Okay. Get him back to his cell."

* * * * *

A policeman opened the door to Sloan's office for John Sacks, and they walked in. The policeman gestured to Sacks. "This is Wellstone's lawyer."

Sloan told the policeman to leave. "Have a seat," Sloan said. "I have some questions about your client." "First, I'd like to know what he's charged with."

"Suspicion of murder."

"Based on what evidence?"

"There is evidence that a wolf has killed people. Four of my officers saw him change from a wolf into a human being."

"If my client is a wolf—and I doubt it because he's been a friend for years—but if he is, how do you know it was he who killed those people?"

"That's why we need to question him."

"You'll have to charge him first. And we both know that suspicion of murder won't hold up. Nothing ties him to those killings." "All right. We don't know for sure that he killed those people."

"Criminals. It killed criminals."

"I know. And I have mixed emotions. He leaned forward toward Sacks and almost whispered. "I never said this, okay? But if he is the wolf that killed those bastards, I think we should pin a medal on the son-of-a-bitch. But that's not how the Commissioner sees it. He doesn't like people—or wolves, or who-knows-what—taking the law into their own hands".

"I understand, and I sympathize with your dilemma. But you don't know if my client killed anyone."

"That's true. But I want him examined and put under observation."

"Only if he consents. And I guarantee that he won't."

"We've got to find out what's going on with him. He could be a danger to people, a danger to himself. We've got to examine him and keep an eye on him."

"Only if he consents. Now, where do I post his bail?"

An hour later, Sloan's phone rings. It's Thatcher, and he's mad.

"I hope what I heard is wrong, because if it's not, your ass is in a sling. You had a wolfman, or whatever the hell it is, in custody and released it?"

"I had no choice. His lawyer bailed him out, and we had nothing to hold him on."

Bullshit! You can always find something to charge someone with. Any rookie knows that. You're on suspension. Without pay."

"Wait! Wait just a fucking minute. You're suspending me because I followed the law, because I didn't cook up some phony charge?"

"You got it."

"You can't do that. I'll take it to the police board."

"Take it where you like. You're on suspension, as of now."

Thatcher hangs up. Sloan slams down the phone.

CHAPTER EIGHT

Troy opened the door of his condominium to Barbara.

"Hi, Barb. Come in and tell me what's on your mind. You sounded upset on the phone."

Barbara entered the living room. She didn't look directly at him.

"Not really upset. But we need to talk."

"About the serum?

"Yes," she said and ran her fingers through her hair. "And no. Something else, too."

Troy gestured to the sofa and Barbara sat. He walked to the bar on the other side of the room.

"Brandy?"

"Yes, please, thanks."

Troy pours two brandies.

"Troy, we've got to talk."

Troy hurried back, gave her the drink and sat next to her.

"So, what's going on?"

Barbara took a gulp of brandy.

She stood and paced back and forth several times, then stopped, and looked away from Troy. "Where do I start? I'm edgy, afraid of what you'll say."

"What could I say to worry you?"

"It's about us. I want to know … need to know if you still have any feelings for me."

"Why?"

She turned to face Troy. "Because I have feelings for you." She cleared her throat. "I sensed it right away when we first met about the notes. I lied to you."

"About what?"

"About being over you. I'm not."

"I thought knowing what I am would …"

"It did. Believe me, it did. But the more we see each other, the less it matters."

"I don't know if this …"

"You know, Troy, I've been with other men since we split. They were handsome, educated, financially stable. But I couldn't connect with them. The relationships were empty."

"I know what you mean. I've had the same experience."

Barbara sat next to him on the sofa. She took another sip of brand y and looked him directly in his eyes.

"The truth is … the truth is, I never stopped loving you."

"Even knowing what I am?"

"I knew you first as Troy Wellstone, the man who probably saved my life, and the guy I fell in love with. That's who you are to me now, too. It's how I'll always see you."

"It's not how you see me. It's what I am—part man and part wolf.

"I don't care. I still love you. I can't help it. I wouldn't care if you were half man and half elephant."

Troy laughed and she laid her head on his shoulder. "Troy, could you ever love me again?"

Troy lifted Barbara's head and pulled her close.

"I already do. As much as I did before."

They kissed passionately.

* * * * *

Troy lied in bed with Barbara curled in his arms.

Barbara smiled. "Some things never change."

"What do you mean?"

"The birth control routine. You'd insist I use the pill and wear an IUD." She laughed. "And you'd still put on a condom."

Troy grinned. "Yeah. We have to be careful."

"Well, that solves a mystery."

"What's that?"

"Why you broke up with me. I could never figure it out. It was because of what you are, wasn't it?"

"I wish I had known then. It would have made things a lot easier. It was the not understanding why you did it that tortured me."

"I'm sorry. If it helps, I was in pretty sad shape, too."

"Really?"

"Yep. Took quite a while to get past it. And, like you, I don't think I ever did."

He gave her a light kiss. "Anyway, let's not talk about it. We're back together and that's what counts. Besides, I've got to get a few hours sleep. I go on patrol soon."

Barbara looked surprised. "Really? Just a few hours?"

"That's all we need to be fully rested. One of the few benefits of being a werewolf."

"That's quite a benefit. Maybe I should become a werewolf. Come over here and bite me."

"I wouldn't recommend that."

CHAPTER NINE

Troy's pack was in the living room of the cabin. "We'll have to be careful," Troy said. "The police are on alert. They'll probably set more traps."

"Maybe we should work in pairs," Hannah said. "like when there's a full moon and the evil ones are out. We can cover each other."

John shook his head. "That dilutes our range. We won't be able to cover as much of the territory."

"We'll have to pair up soon anyway," Hannah replied. "The full moon is a few days away."

Troy nodded. "Yeah, you're right."

"How do the others operate?" Kevin asked.

"Just like in the movies," Troy answered. "They're malicious murderers. They kill babies."

"Really?"

"Not to mention pregnant women," Troy said.

"Pregnant women? Babies? Why?"

"They believe devouring young flesh and blood maintains their youth and strength. Last month, they killed a young couple walking through a park. The mother was pregnant. She had a young boy with her, and the father was pushing a baby in a carriage. Three wolves swooped down on them."

Kevin looked confused. "Why aren't the cops after them?"

"We think it's because the evil ones are only out one or two nights a month," Tom explained. "The cops may not even know they exist."

"They've got to be suspicious when they find all those chewed up bodies," Kevin said.

"The evil ones usually bury the bodies in the woods," Tom responded. "Sometimes they're scared away by something and leave the bodies behind. But that's not the norm."

"We think the cops assume the people were killed by a large dog or regular wolf or coyote," Miriam said.

"Why do the evil ones attack us?"

"Pardon the pun," Julia said, "but it's in their blood."

"Right," Troy said. He looked at Kevin. "Kev, this is your first patrol when the evil ones are out. So, we'll put you in a three-pack, you and me and Julia."

Kevin looked at Julia, then at Troy. "I'd feel better if …"

Troy put his hand on Kevin's shoulder. "Don't

worry. Julia is as powerful as you and I. All the ladies are."

Kevin turned at the women. "Sorry. No offense intended."

Julia smiled. "None taken."

* * * * *

A bright full moon lightened the path of the forest preserve where Troy, Kevin, and Julia were patrolling. They sniffed the air.

"They're here," Julia whispered.

"I know," Troy said. "I picked up the scent too. How about you, Kev?"

"Yeah. It's faint, but I've got it.

"Okay," Troy said. "Let's fan out in wolf form, but keep each other in sight."

They transformed and spread out. Troy crawled forward. The others did the same. Ahead of him, Troy saw two wolves stalking them. To his right were two more, and together they attacked.

Troy leapt and bit into the neck of the closest wolf. Another jumped toward Troy, but Julia caught it in midair and chewed it's throat. Kevin struggled with the last two. Troy killed his foe, then went for one of those attacking Kevin and killed it. The remaining evil wolf ran away. Troy noticed Julia saw bleeding from her right rear leg. He licked the wound, then went to human form. Kevin and Julia also transformed.

Troy asked Julia if she was okay. "Yeah. That bite went pretty deep, but I should be all right."

"Good. But that's it for you tonight."

"No. I can keep going."

"Julia, you're wounded. Leave and let Hannah patch you up. I don't want to worry about you. It might break my concentration."

"Okay. You're right."

"Let's get her back to her car," Troy told Kevin.

Julia shook her head. "No, I can make it."

"I don't want you on your own. There'll be more of them looking for revenge. We've got to stay together."

They walked alongside her, holding her arms. Then, they stopped and sniffed.

"They're back already?" Troy asked.

A group of six wolves appeared. Troy and the others went to wolf form. But the pack approached slowly, then stopped, except for the leader, who neared Troy. They sniffed each other and seemed to communicate, nodding and shaking their heads. Troy went to human form.

"All right," Troy said. "A truce. I don't think it's possible, but I'll meet your envoy tomorrow night.

The Devil's Canyon Forest Preserve is fine. I'll be in the parking lot at nine."

The other wolf nodded, and stepped back. Then he and his pack turned and ran away. Julia and Kevin took human form.

"He wants a truce?" Julia asked.

"Yeah. Said he'll send an envoy to meet me."

"Be careful, Troy," Julia said, "It could be a trick."

CHAPTER TEN

Troy was in his car in the faintly illuminated parking lot, his arm hanging out of the opened window. The lot was deserted and the forest was eerily quiet except for an occasional coyote howling or an owl hooting. He was suddenly startled as a bat screeched and flapped past him.

He scanned the area, saw movement in the bushes in front of him. He tensed as he saw two glowing eyes, then relaxed as the coyote scampered away. Minutes later, headlights swept along the trees and bushes as a car pulled into the parking lot and parked next to him. Troy looked at the driver, who opened his passenger side window.

"You the envoy?" Troy asked.

"Yeah. You the pack leader?"

"Yes."

Troy gestured with his hand. "Come on over. Let's see if we can arrange something."

The envoy got out of his car and went into Troy's.

"Why didn't your leader come?" Troy asked.

"You might recognize him, and he doesn't want that. My name is Ray."

"Call me Troy."

"I'm glad you agreed to meet."

"I'm always willing to listen."

"Good. We'd like a truce with your pack. There's no point in continuing to kill each other. Leave us alone and we'll do the same. It's as simple as that.

"I'm afraid it's not. You kill people. We protect them."

"Look, the streets are yours any time you like. We're only out when the moon is full."

"You've got a big pack. What, maybe thirty or more?"

Ray smiles. "Nice try. But I won't divulge that. We're a larger pack than yours is all I'll say because you already know that."

"All right. That was a bit clumsy. But the point is that you can kill a lot of people in a few nights."

"Okay. How about this? Attack us only when we're threatening a human. Some of you pounced on four of my pack a last night and killed three of them. We won't …"

"Wrong. They attacked us and we defended ourselves."

"That's not what I heard."

"He said. She said. Believe what you like. But you know that's not how we operate."

"I thought you were ready to listen. But not with a very open mind."

"That's because we have no more choice in what we do than you."

Ray leaned back and sighed. "Yeah. I can't argue with that. Ah! I knew this was futile. But I thought it was worth a shot. You nailed it right away. We're hard-wired. You do good and we're wicked. To be honest, I envy you."

"Why?"

"You know, some of the myths about werewolves aren't myths at all. The fact is, we don't like what we are and what we do. It's agonizing."

"Do others like you feel the same?"

"Most of them. There are some—like our pack leader—who revel in it. But most of us are tortured. Some have committed suicide."

"I guess I can understand that."

"Well, there's nothing left to say. Too bad we couldn't work something out."

Ray started to get out of the car. Troy said, "What if I want to talk to you again?"

Ray turned around. "About what?"

"You never know. We're working on … I may think of something."

Ray took out his wallet, pulled out a card and handed it to Troy.

CHAPTER ELEVEN

Kevin walked into Troy's office and sat across the desk.

"Okay, what's on your mind?" Troy said.

Kevin's jaws were clenched. He turned away for a moment and then back to Troy. "I've been dating a girl and I don't know how to handle it. I don't know how it happened, Troy. It just did. Even after what you told me. I fell in love with her and she feels the same."

Troy grimaced. "I'm not sure I'm the right person for advice. Look at me and Barb."

"I know. That's why I'm here. How did you deal with it?"

"Not very well, obviously. I broke up with her, but the minute I saw her again, I was overwhelmed."

"Sure. But it was a quirk of fate that you had to meet her again. Would you have stayed away from her if it hadn't been for that?"

"I honestly don't know. I thought about her a lot."

"Yeah. I can't get her out of my mind. Every time I

leave her I can't wait to see her again." Troy paused and squeezed the bridge of his nose. "The truth is, I don't know what to tell you. The right thing to do is break off with her. You know that. But that's easier said than done."

"That it is. I'll have to think of something. Well, thanks for talking about this with me."

* * * * *

Watch Commander Alan Sloan sat in Troy's office. "This an official visit?" Troy asked. "I thought everything was taken care of.

"Semi-official. I need some information from you. I'll get right to the point. I think you *are* a werewolf."

"Why doesn't that surprise me?"

"I didn't see you change from a wolf into a man, but four of my cops did. And there have been other incidents of a wolf attacking criminals."
"Yeah. I've heard about that."

"Listen, if you're getting the bad guys, I'm okay with that. I'd like to work with you and there are other cops who feel the same."

Troy pursed his lips. "Commander Sloan, if I responded to that …"

Sloan held up his hands. "Understood. You'd just about be confessing to be what I think you are. Give it some thought. There may be ways to coordinate our efforts and share information."

"There's really nothing more I can tell you."

Sloan took a card from his shirt pocket and handed it to Troy. "If you change your mind, give me a call. My home number is on the back. I'll have time on my hands for a while. The Commissioner suspended me for releasing you."

Troy's eyebrows furrowed. "That doesn't seem right. He must have been pretty pissed off." Troy leaned forward and studied Sloan. "Tell me about the Commissioner. Does he fly off the handle often?"

"Not really. But he's under pressure at times and loses it."

"He married?"

"No. He dated, still does once in a while, but never tied the knot with anyone."

"How old is he."

"I think mid-fifties."

"Healthy?"

"Yeah. He's very fit. Works out a lot." Troy steepled his fingers over his lips.

"He take much time off?"

"Maybe one or two days a month. Why? Is that important?"

"Could be."

Troy turned the calendar on his desk toward Sloan.

"Do you remember the last time he took off?

Troy pointed to two dates on the calendar. "Was it these two dates?

"Yeah, I think so."

Troy glanced at his wristwatch. "Pardon me. Commander, but I have two important meetings to attend. But I may have some information for you soon. "

CHAPTER TWELVE

Troy was in the dining room of the cabin with John, Tom, Hannah and Julia. After eating, Troy described his meeting with Sloan. "He seems genuine. He's convinced I'm a werewolf. But for all he knows I'm the only one."

"Anything else?"

Troy leaned forward as if about to reveal a secret. "Yeah. Remember, I told you the envoy said that most of the evil pack hates what they are? But some of them enjoy what they do."

Julia seemed suspicious. "And?"

"Well," Troy continued, "the pack leader didn't meet with me because he thought I might recognize him."

"So," Hannah said, "he's got to be a somebody, a celebrity or a public figure, like the mayor."

"Not quite that high up," Troy answered. "But how about the Police Commissioner?"

Tom shrugged. "Why do you think that?"

"Look how he reacted to Sloan saying they should leave the wolf alone. And how he suspended Sloan for releasing me."

"That's not enough," Diana said. "Maybe he's just a straight-laced, by-the-book cop who doesn't like people—or, in our case, wolves—taking the law into their own hands."

"Could be," Troy said. "Just the same, his reaction to what Sloan said and did was extreme."

"What difference does that make?" John asked.

"By itself, nothing," Troy responded. "But the Commissioner—even though Sloan says he's very fit —takes a few days off every month. Sloan showed me the last dates the Commissioner took off."

Troy was silent for a moment, increasing the tension in the room. Then, "They were nights with a full moon."

They suck in their breaths and their eyes widened.

"Good lord," John gasped. "You may be on to something, Troy. And if you're right, we've got a boatload of problems. He could set the whole police force on us."

* * * * *

Troy, Tom and Kevin were having lunch in Troy's office. Kevin wiped his mouth with a paper napkin. "I've got a question. I've been with the pack for six months, and I noticed that Barry hasn't been out with us during a full moon since I joined the pack.

"He doesn't patrol during full moons," Tom answered.

"Why not?"

Troy swallowed the last bite of his corned beef sandwich. "When he was seventeen, Barry got his girlfriend pregnant. He married her, and she had the child, a boy, named Daniel. Given the bad start, they pretty much lived happily ever after."

"Until Barry's werewolf genes kicked in," Tom continued. "He was in a bind. He couldn't continue patrolling to protect people, as he was compelled to do, and raise his family. In the end, he thought the best thing to do was leave his wife and son, although he sent them money on a regular basis."

Kevin squinted. "That still bothers him?"

Troy shook his head. "No. It's not that. The boy turned twenty-one almost a year ago and Barry is worried he might have developed into an evil werewolf."

"What if he does?" Kevin asked.

"That's the big question," Troy said. "He knows what he should do, but that doesn't mean he will. He's tortured by it."

"I would be too," Kevin replied. "How can you kill your own son? I feel guilty just killing criminals. How does he keep track of the kid?"

"That's why he's not with us during full moons," Tom said. "He stakes out the son's house to see if Daniel has become a werewolf, especially an evil one. It's all right with us. It's only a few nights a month and it's very important to him."

CHAPTER THIRTEEN

Troy sat at the conference table in his office with Tom, Miriam, Diana, Julia, and Barry.

"All right," Troy said. "What's on your minds?"

"It's about the serum," Tom said.

"Barb says she's sure she's on the right track. She should …"

"That's not exactly what we're here to talk about," Diana said.

Troy looked at them curiously. "What then?"

They sat quietly for a few moments, then Barry spoke. "We don't want to use the serum."

Troy smiled. "Well, doesn't that beat all?"

Miriam leaned to Troy. "It's not that we don't appreciate what Barbara is doing, it's …"

Troy held up his hands. "You don't have to say any more. I feel the same, have almost from the start. But I didn't say it because I didn't want to influence anyone."

"I feel guilty about it," Tom said. "It's like I'm running away from my responsibility to protect people."

"Yeah," Troy said. "I think that's it. We should have talked about this a long time ago."

"I guess we were too ecstatic to think objectively about it," Diana said.

Tom leaned forward. "Well, at least we finally got a conscience call. Better late than never. What about Kevin and John and Hannah?

"I'd bet they feel the same," Julia said.

Miriam looked at Troy. "I'll call Hannah and meet her for lunch. Will you contact Kevin and John?"

"Yeah," Troy answered. "I'll take care of that."

"Poor Barbara," Diana said. "She put so much into this."

"I think she'll understand," Troy said.

"Don't want to be nosey," Tom inquired, "but how are things with you and Barbara?

Troy shrugged and spread his hands. "What can I say? We're back to where we were. I fought it, but our feelings are just too strong."

Julia's looked shocked. "Have you …?"

"Yes. We've made love."

Julia's face flushed. "That's wrong, Troy. It's just plain wrong. It's dangerous. What if she …"

"Don't worry, Julia. That's not going to happen."

"It's still wrong."

Troy's looked irritated. "Maybe. But it's happened and I'm not going to break up with her again. So, why don't we just let this drop?"

Troy glanced at the others. "Anything else?"

They shook their heads.

"Okay. I guess we're done."

They left. Troy returned to his desk and began proofreading an article. A few minutes later, Julia returned and closed the door behind her.

Troy looked up at her. "What's on your mind?"

"I think you know."

"Barbara?"

"That's right. You shouldn't be doing this. It's …"

"Relax. Nothing awful is going to happen. Besides, it's a personal matter."

"I don't think so. It could affect the pack. If she got pregnant …"

"She won't!" "

You're that much in love with her that you'd take the chance?"

"I guess so."

Julia's face tightened. "What about me? Why didn't you take the chance with me?'

Troy gave her a dismissive look. "Julia, that ended a long time ago. There's no point in rehashing it. I thought it was over."

Julia stiffened. "Not for me."

Troy looked astonished. "Are you serious? I thought it was a clean break with no hard feelings. You never said or showed anything."

"No, I didn't. Pride I guess. And now you're in love with her again. She's not even one of us. What if you *did* break up and she told the police about us out of spite?"

"She'd never do that."

"How can you be so sure?"

"I know her, Julia. She'd never do that, no matter what."

She looked at him contemptuously, eyes narrowed and jaw muscles squeezed. "You going to tell he about us not wanting the serum?"

"Tomorrow."

"Great. Be sure you fuck her brains out to make her feel better."

Troy grimaced. "What a crude, disgusting remark! How could ..."

"You think that was crude and disgusting? I'll tell you what's really crude and disgusting."

She leaned forward, her eyes bulged, her lips pulled back, showing her teeth. "I was pregnant with your baby when you threw me aside."

Troy is stunned.

"What? Pregnant? My baby?

"That's right!"

"Well, what …"

Still scowling, she stood erect with her hands on her hips. "What happened to it? I aborted it!"

Troy's jaw dropped. Neither he nor Julia spoke for a few moments. Troy glared at Julia, his jaws clenched. "You should have talked to me before you did that, Julia. That was my baby, too. We should have made the decision together."

"Why? What was I supposed to do, keep it and spend the next twenty years wondering what it would become? We'd be like Barry."

"I know, but you still should have talked to me. Come to think of it, why are you telling me now?"

Julia scoffed. "Figure that out yourself."

Troy hesitated, thinking. "I have. It was to sting me, wasn't it? To get back at me for being involved with Barbara again.

Julia stayed silent, but a small, almost unnoticeable, smile creased her lips.

"Did doing this, this revenge, make you feel better?" Troy asked.

Julia smiled wickedly. "A little. But not near enough."

CHAPTER FOURTEEN

Troy was in a booth at the far end of an upscale hotel bar and signaled Sloan when he walked in. He stood, they shook hands, greeted each other and sat down.

Troy stared at Sloan. "I hope you're not wearing a wire or anything like that. I want this to be confidential."

Sloan shook his head. "No wires, no parabolic mics. Nothing. This is between us."

"Maybe I shouldn't just take your word for it, but this is imperative, so it's worth a chance."

Troy took a deep breath. "Okay. You're right. I am a werewolf."

They stopped talking as the waitress takes their orders.

"I can prove it if you like," Troy said. "Not here, of course, but …"

"No need for that. I believe you. But I've got questions. Were you born this way?

"All right. One thing at a time. I'll tell you everything."

* * * * *

"That's a hell of a story," Sloan said. "Especially the evil wolves. They really are a menace to society. And you said your pack is badly outnumbered."

Trod nodded. "Yes, but we've learned to deal with that. And we have advantages over them that I'll tell you about later." He hesitated.

"The last time we talked, you said we might work together."

"I remember that. But it was to stop criminals, to prevent crime."

"That's fine by me. But how about working together to get rid of the evil ones? They're criminals. You just said they were a threat to society."

Sloan thought for a moment. "That's true. And I'm open to that, too."

"Okay. I've got an idea. Let's do what your Commissioner did to me."

"Set a trap for them?"

"Yeah, use decoys. A man and a woman. They'd have to be ordinary humans. The evil pack would sense it if they were one of ours. When the evil ones attack, we hit them."

"Could work. I know cops who'd go along with that."

CHAPTER FIFTEEN

Troy and Barbara were on a sofa in her living room sipping glasses of wine.

"So," she said." What's up? Why did you have to see me?"

She put her wine glass on the coffee table and cozied up to him. "Not that I mind, but you look conflicted."

"Not conflicted. Confused. Embarrassed maybe."

"About what? Is it about us?"

Troy sighed. "It's about the serum."

She looked relieved. "Oh, that's coming along well. It's just a matter of …"

"You're going to think I'm crazy; that my whole pack is whacko."

"Why, Troy? Get to the point."

"I came over because I wanted to tell you in person."

"Tell me what?"

"That we don't want to use the serum."

Barbara's eyes widened. "What? Why not? I put my heart and soul into that. And now you don't want it?"

"I know, and I'm sorry, Barb."

Barbara stood. "For what reason?"

Troy sighed. "Diana called it. If … if we take the serum, we're giving up our responsibility to protect people. She said she'd feel guilty. I guess I would, too."

"I see."

"It's who we are, Barb. It's, I suppose, our purpose, our duty. We can't run away from it. Can you understand?"

"I don't know, Troy" She paused. "I guess so. Kind of. You're a principled, ethical man. And your pack seems to be the same. So, yeah, I can live with that."

Troy leaned over and kissed her on the cheek. "Thanks. I figured you would."

"But why go on with the serum? What's the point?"

"You work won't be wasted. If we can get at least some of the evil werewolves to use it, we could save lives that they'd otherwise take."

* * * * *

Kevin stepped into Troy's office and sat down.

"What's up," he asked. Why did you want to see me?

"How are things with your girlfriend?"

Kevin bowed his head. "I broke up with her the other night."

"Ah, Kevin, I'm sorry. I'm really sorry. I know how you're suffering."

Tears formed in Kevin's eyes. He cleared his throat. "Thanks. I'll get over it. It'll just take some time."

"That's right. It may a while, but you'll get past it.

"I suppose. But I already miss her."

"Try to keep it out of your mind. Concentrate on your work.

"I will."

CHAPTER SIXTEEN

Hannah rang Miriam's doorbell. She waited a few seconds and rang again. A minute passed and she knocked hard on the door. "Jenny. Jenny, open the door."

Finally, the door opened. Hannah held up a bag. "I brought you soup. Troy said you called in sick the last three days. What is it, the flu?"

Miriam looked dazed and just stood there for a few moments.

"Yeah. I think so."

Miriam's eyes were dilated. She was sweating and flushed. Hannah studied her.

"Miriam don't tell me that you're on that junk again."

Miriam turned away, stepped to the sofa and sat. Hannah followed.

"Miriam, for god's sake, tell me you're not on that fucking heroin again."

Hannah grabbed Miriam's arm and turned it over. Needle marks. Hannah dropped her head and tears welled in her eyes. She put her arms around Miriam.

Hannah's voice cracked. "Oh, Miriam. Why? It's been almost three years. And now you're back on that shit again."

Hannah stood and stepped back. Now, her face was red with anger, and she shouted, "How could you! How dare you! After all I did for you to break that habit. After what the whole pack did for you."

Hannah's head dropped. She took a deep breath and sat back on the sofa next to Miriam. She sighed heavily. Miriam put her hand on Hannah's.

Miriam's voice was weak and slow. "I'm sor … sorry. I'm sorry. Let you down. Let everybody down. Especially you. You did the most."

Hannah put her arm around Miriam.

"Okay. Let's get you to bed and have you sleep this off."

*　*　*　*　*

Troy pulled up to the cabin, got out and entered. Hannah and Miriam were on a sofa. Hannah's eyes widened. Miriam was slumped on the sofa semi-conscious.

"Troy," Hannah said. "What are you doing here?"

"A better question is what you two are doing here."

Troy saw a syringe and a rubber tourniquet on the sofa next to Miriam.

"Good lord, Hannah. What the hell is going on?"

Hannah bowed her head. "I'm sorry, Troy. But she was in a bad way. I've never seen her like that before. She needed a fix. I couldn't refuse. I just couldn't."

Troy approached Hannah. "Of all people, you should know this is wrong. It only makes things worse for her."

"I caught her doing it herself. She must have gotten it from a dealer she knew before. We're close, Troy. We're like sisters. Better she got it from me than using the shit that's on the street."

Miriam stirred. Her eyelids fluttered and half opened. "Oh. Troy. Ha … how are you?"

She started to sit up, but flopped back down and dozed off.

"I'm sorry, Troy. I thought I could give her the heroin and gradually wean her off of it."

"Yeah? How's that working?"

"It's not. The more she gets, the more she wants."

"We've got to get her back into treatment."

CHAPTER SEVENTEEN

Kevin sat in a cocktail lounge. He leaned on the bar, head and shoulders slumped. He finished his drink and ordered another.

"You got a problem?" the bartender asked.

"It's personal. Why?"

"You're putting these down pretty fast." Another customer at the end of the bar snickered and in slurred words said, "He needs to get laid."

Kevin's face reddened. "Who asked you?"

"You need to get laid."

"Maybe he's right," the bartender said with a grin. "Maybe you should go home to your wife and get laid."

"Not married."

"Okay, how 'bout your girlfriend?" the customer teased. "Don't you got a girlfriend?"

Kevin sneered. "I think you should stay out of this!"

"When was the last time you banged your girl-friend?"

"Fuck off!"

"The way you're acting, she must be holding out on you for a long time. You must have really pissed her off."

Kevin jumped to his feet and rushed to the customer. He grabbed him by the throat, lifted him and slammed him against the wall.

"Shut up! Shut up or I'll tear your fucking throat out!"

A few women screamed and ran outside. Others followed. The bartender came from behind the bar.

"Cut it out!" the bartender yelled. "Stop it, you crazy bastard!"

The bartender grabbed Kevin around the neck from behind. Kevin shoved his elbow into the bartender's rib cage twice. The bartender huffed, doubled over, and his grip around Kevin's neck loosened. Kevin snatched one of the bartender's wrists, twisted it behind the bartender's back, and put him into a hammer lock. Kevin pushed him back to the bar, put his hand on the back of the bartender's head and slammed it into the bar twice. The bartender crumbled.

Then, Kevin went back to the customer and drove a hard right hand into the customer's stomach. The customer gasped and fell to the floor.

The bartender was unconscious on the floor. Kevin walked back to his drink, guzzled it down and walked out.

CHAPTER EIGHTEEN

Barry walked into Troy's office and slumped into a chair. There were tears in his eyes.

"Barry. What's the matter?"

He said nothing for a few minutes. Then his voice quivered. "He's one of them "He's an evil one."

Troy's jaws dropped. "Oh, Barry, I'm sorry—" Barry sobbed. Troy got up and sat in the chair next to him.

"Try to control yourself," Troy said. Then, "No, don't. Get it out of your system. Go ahead. Cry, yell. Whatever."

Barry tried to talk but couldn't. Finally he said, "Last night. I saw him last night."

"How do you know he's an evil one? Maybe …" Barry shook his head. "Just after dark, he came out of the house and ran off. I followed him and he joined four others. They weren't ours."

Troy sat back, thinking.

"What if it's another pack like us? It's possible, Barry. Isn't it?"

"No."

"Why?"

"After I first saw him, I checked for three nights when there was no full moon. He didn't show. He only came out during the full moon."

Troy put his hand on Barry's shoulder. "Barry, if there's anything I can do, if there's anything any of us can do, you only need to ask."

"I know. Thank you"

* * * * *

Troy stepped into Tom's office looking concerned. Tom and Diana were working on a page layout. They looked up.

"What's the matter, Troy? Tom asked. "You look flustered."

"I am. Kevin's been arrested."

Simultaneously, Tom and Diana shout, "What!" Why?" Diana asked. "What did he do?"

"Involuntary manslaughter."

"Good lord," Diana said. "What happened?"

"He got into a fight. Hit a guy hard in the stomach. Turned out the guy had a cardiac condition. The punch caused a heart attack and he died."

Diana dropped her head. Tom put an arm around her.

"I just talked to John. He's on his way to the police station. I'm going to meet him. Tom, contact the others, would you?

"Sure thing."

* * * * *

Troy, John and Kevin walked out of the police station to the parking lot.

Kevin looked at John. "Thanks for bailing me out, John."

"No problem. But you've got to watch that temper."

"It's not so much anger. I'm just sad and lonely."

"Anything I can do?" Troy asked.

"Nah. I'll just go back to my place and work my way through it."

Troy rubbed the back of his neck. "I'm not up for going back to work. Think I'll go to the cabin and relax. If you need me, let me know."

* * * * *

Troy was with Barry in the office conference room.

"Tomorrow night is a full moon," Barry said.

"What are you thinking?" Troy asked.

"I'm going to do what I have to. He's an evil one, and I've got to kill him like I'd kill any other evil wolf.

"Good god, Barry, I can't imagine what you're going through. Would you like me to go with you to back you up?"

"I can't ask that of you."

"You're not asking. I'm offering."

Barry hesitated, then saidm, "That's not a bad idea. Thanks."

* * * * *

Troy and Barry, in wolf form, hid near Barry's son's home. Just after sundown, a werewolf left the house. Barry and Troy approached it. It spun toward them growling, teeth bared ears back, tail up. Suddenly, Barry took human form.

"Daniel!" Barry shouted. "Danny, wait. Please listen to me. I'm your father. I left a long time ago. But I'm your father."

Daniel lunged at Barry and knocked him down. Troy went after Daniel and they fought. Barry went to wolf form—and attacked Troy. Troy took on both of them but was bitten in his shoulder. He backed off, then turned and ran away.

* * * * *

Troy sat on a sofa in the living room of the cabin with Tom, Hanna, and Diana. His shirt was off, and his shoulder was bandaged.

"It looked worse than it was," Hannah said. "It'll heal quickly."

"Thanks," Troy said.

"So, now that you're fixed up," Tom said. "What do we do about Barry?"

Troy shook his head. "I'm stumped. But we've got to contact him somehow."

Hannah taped the bandage, "I still can't get my mind around what he did."

"I can't judge him. I'm not a father. Maybe his paternal instincts were too much for him."

CHAPTER NINETEEN

Tom walked into Troy's office. "Have you heard from Kevin?" he asked. "One of our advertisers called and asked about him. I haven't seen or talked to him in three days."

"No, I haven't either."

"I called him a few times, but he doesn't answer."

Troy scratched his cheek. "I'll take a run over to his place and see what's going on."

Tom pursed his lips. "Good. Keep me posted."

* * * * *

Troy rang Kevin's bell three times. No answer. He knocked on the door. "Kevin. Are you in there? Kev. Come to the door."

Nothing.

Troy walked to another door and rang the bell. In a few moments, a man answered.

"What can I do for you?"

"Does the manager live here?

"Yeah. Second floor. Room two oh seven. Why?"

"Probably nothing." He pointed to Kevin's apartment. "But I need to get into that apartment."

* * * * *

Troy and the apartment manager, a middle-aged blonde woman, walked to Kevin's apartment, she held a set of keys on a chain.

"Maybe we should call the cops." she said.

"Not yet. We many not need to."

The manager opened the door and Troy stepped in. The manager stayed at the door nibbling her lower lip. Troy moved through the apartment, looked cautiously first around the living and dining room. Then he peeked into the bedroom. No Kevin. Finally, he entered the bathroom. And the first thing he noticed was the blood. Blood all over.

Troy took a deep breath and he slowly peeled back the shower curtain.

Kevin's body lay curled up in a fetal position. Both his wrists were slashed. Troy felt for a neck pulse, already knowing that there wouldn't be any. He stepped out to the manager.

"Okay. Call the police."

* * * * *

Troy, Tom, and Diana sat in the living room looking stupefied. "John is making the arrangements with Hannah," Troy said.

"Why on earth would he do that?" Diana asked. "He hadn't even gone to trial. And he was out on bail."

"Something else was going on with him."

"Yes, there was," Troy said. "Two things. He felt guilty about killing people. He was depressed about it and couldn't adapt, couldn't accept it."

Diana eyes protruded. "But we only kill—"

"I know," Troy said. "I talked to him about it more than once. It didn't help."

"The second reason?" Tom asked.

"He was in love. And he broke up with her. I guess you both know why."

Diana closed her eyes and shook her head. "Sometimes, being what we are is a curse."

CHAPTER TWENTY

Troy opened the cabin door for Sloan and four other police officers.

"Welcome to our den," Troy said. "Come in and meet the pack."

They entered the living room and his pack stood to greet them and shook hands.

Sloan introduced the officers. They were Nick Dawson, Jeff Atkins and Mike Bartello.

Sloan gestures toward a female officer. "And this, believe it or not, is officer Kathleen Wolfe."

They laughed.

"These are the ones who nabbed you," Sloan told Troy. "They saw you change from a wolf into a man, so they're believers and you can trust them."

"That's good to hear," Troy said. "Have a seat."

They all did. "Your plan is good," Sloan said. "The park you picked for the ambush is fine. Not much pedestrian traffic and poorly lit. We'll have Jeff and Kathy walk down the path as lures."

"Good," Troy said. "There are benches where Jeff and Miss Wolfe can sit. Keep your men hidden in the woods near them.

"Sounds fine," Wolfe said.

"We'll be nearby," Troy said. "If something happens, we'll be there in no time."

Troy hesitated for a moment. "There's something else. I didn't tell you before because I wasn't sure I wanted you to know. It's about the Commissioner."

"What about him?"

"We're pretty certain he's the leader of the evil pack."

Sloan's head snapped back. "What! Are you serious?"

As a heart attack."

"Why do you think that?"

"A number of reasons, but the most important is that the days he took off were nights with a full moon."

Sloan's eyes bulged. "That's got to be more than coincidence."

"Good lord," Wolfe said. "The highest-ranking cop is a werewolf? That's mind boggling."

"It's chilling," said Sloan. "Okay. I'll buy it for now, but I'll have to check this out thoroughly.

Sloan stood and the officers followed suit.

Sloan shook Troy's hand. "We're going to leave now. I just wanted you all to meet each other.

"Fine. Next Saturday is a full moon. We'll be there at sundown."

* * * * *

Troy was relaxing on the couch in his condo when the phone rang. He picked it up.

"Hello."

"Is this Troy Wellstone?" someone asked.

"Yes, it is. Who is this?"

"I'm Dr. Neil Hamilton at Christ Advocate Hospital. Do you know a Barry Goldman?"

"Yes, I do. What about him?"

"He was brought into the emergency room a few nights ago chewed up pretty badly. We don't know by what."

"How did you find me? And why now?"

"He had no identification on him, and he only just regained consciousness and told us who to call."

* * * * *

Troy walked into Barry's hospital room. Barry was bandaged on his face, neck and arms. He had IVs in one arm. The heart monitor beeped and a blood pressure cuff occasionally inflated.

"How you holding up, Barry?"

"I guess I'll live."

"What happened?"

"He turned on me. Daniel turned on me."

Tears flowed down his cheeks. "After you got away, he attacked me."

"I'm sorry, Barry."

"No. I'm the one who's sorry, Troy. For attacking you. You came to help, and I turned on you."

"Don't think about that now."

"I can't help it. I'm going to leave the pack. I don't deserve to be a part of it."

"Don't be silly. You'll always be part of us."

"I couldn't help it, Troy. I couldn't hurt him, and I couldn't let you hurt him either.

"I understand. Don't trouble yourself. What happened? How did you get here?"

"Somebody must have called the police. They got an ambulance and that's all I remember until I woke up this morning."

"Well, you just relax and get well. The others will be around to visit."

CHAPTER TWENTY-ONE

Police Commissioner Ken Thatcher knocked on the door Barbara's home. He was in uniform, as were the two officers with him. Barbara looked through the peek hole and opened the door.

"Miss Lane? Barbara Lane?"

"Yes. I'm Barbara. How can I help you?"

"May we come in? You might be able to help us find someone."

Barbara stood aside and gestured to the sofa. "Have a seat?"

Thatcher sat on the sofa. The officers remained standing.

"We're looking for Troy Wellstone," Thatcher said. "We believe you know him."

Barbara sat on an easy chair across from them. "Yes, I do. Why do you want to find him?"

"I'm going to tell you something that I think you may already know. If not, you're going to be shocked, but it's true."

"Go ahead. But you're not going to tell me any-thing negative about Troy. He's a good man and—"

"He's more than a man, Miss Lane. He's a wolf, a werewolf."

"How did … how can you think something like that?"

Thatcher gave her a knowing smile. "You knew. Of course, you did."

"I don't know what you're talking—"

"Stop! Don't lie to me."

He stood and approached her. "He's a werewolf and you know it. What you don't know is that so am I, and so are these officers."

"You're one of the evil ones, aren't you?"

"He told you about us?"

"Yes, and I can tell you he'll never agree to any-thing with you. Not even for me."

"We'll see. Right now, you'll have to come with us."

Barbara stood. "Why? Where?"

"You'll know soon enough."

"No! I'm not going anywhere."

One of the policemen grabbed her and put his hand over her mouth as the other slapped on handcuffs on her. She struggled, to no avail. Thatcher reached into his pocket and took out a cellophane-wrapped piece of cloth soaked in chloroform. He unwrapped it and held it over her mouth and nose. She fought the drug for a few moments, then passed out.

* * * * *

Thatcher and the two policemen stood over Barbara, who was lying on a sofa just coming out of her sleep.

"How are you? " Thatcher asked.

Barbara sat up slowly and shook her head. "I'm groggy. And sick to my stomach."

"That won't last long. Now, I want you to behave. If you try to escape or scream, you'll get another taste of that chloroform. You understand?"

"Yes." She looked around.

"Where am I?"

"A small place I keep for situations like this."

Thatcher looked out the window at a setting sun. "We don't have much time. Tell me about Wellstone."

"I don't know what you want to know. I'm only dating the guy. I don't know much about him."

"Come on. He let you know what he is, and he told you about us. He wouldn't have done that if you were just casually dating."

"I can't tell you anything."

Thatcher again looked at his watch. "Okay. Have it your way for now. But this questioning isn't over. We just don't have time right now."

"What do you want from Troy, and why are you holding me?"

"You're a good bargaining chip in a serious negotiation. We tried talking with him, but he refused our offer. With us holding you, he might change his mind."

She glared at him. "This won't work. He won't cooperate."

"When daylight comes, we'll talk again. But now, we're going to transform. I'll leave these two officers with you."

Thatcher and the officers started to transform. They stiffen, their facial features, arms, and legs slowly and painfully took wolf form and thick fur sprouts from their skin. They moaned in pain until the transformation was complete.

Barbara turned away and was about to scream, but one of the wolves leapt on her, his front paws on her thighs, his teeth pressed against her cheek. He jumped down, shook his head back and forth, indicating to her not to her scream. She looked at him, her eyes protruding.

Thatcher communicated with the other wolves. They sat in front of Barbara, and he left. They stared at her and occasionally let out a low growl.

*　*　*　*　*

Troy and the others gathered in the living room going over the planned ambush. "We'll stay a little farther south of the police, but not too far," Troy said. "We've got to be able to get to them instantly if the evil ones attack."

The cabin door opened. Miriam walked in. They're all stunned. Troy jumped to his feet. "What are you doing here? You're supposed to in the hospital being treated."

"I snuck out."

"Miriam," Troy said. "You're not out of the woods yet. It's only been a week. You're supposed to—"

"I'll go back. But tonight, I'm going to fight with my pack."

Troy glared at her. "Out of the question. I'll take you back myself."

"No! I'll fight with my pack tonight! You'll need every one of us. We're outnumbered. I'll go back tomorrow. I promise. But tonight, I'm with all of you."

* * * * *

Sloan and his men were in place, hidden in the woods and brush. Troy's pack was close by, scanning the area. Officers Kathleen Wolfe and Jeff Atkins strolled down a path in the park, then sat on a nearby bench.

Troy spotted movement in bushes behind the two officers. He looked at his pack and whispered, "You all see that?"

They nodded.

"Okay. Go to wolf form."

They did and crept toward the path when four wolves attacked Wolfe and Atkins.

Troy's pack raced to them, but was unexpectedly attacked by eight evil ones, which were concealed in the woods farther down the path.

Wolfe and Atkins opened fire, killing two wolves, but one chewed into Jeff's neck and the other sunk its teeth into Wolfe's abdomen and dragged her away. Sloan and the other officers ran toward the bench and began firing, but they were attacked by five wolves hidden in the bushes to their right.

"Look out!" Sloan shouted. "On the right."

The police fired and killed two evil ones, but the others continued attacking. One ripped out the throat of an officer and another grabbed one of Sloan's arms. Sloan shot and killed it. Another officer killed an evil wolf but was mortally wounded by two more.

Troy heard the shots but could do nothing. His pack was in a fight for its existence. Troy saw Tom get bit in the left rear leg. He limped back, but still fought. Troy sprang at Tom's foe and killed it.

Julia fought ferociously, even though she was bleeding from her neck and chest and one of her ears was half ripped off. Another wolf bit her in the right rear paw. She spun around and attacked it.

Troy's pack and the evil ones fought fiercely. Both took casualties as the combat went on. Despite Julia's wounds, she continued to fight savagely, attacking, counterattacking, and refusing to leave the battle. Two evil ones attacked Miriam. She killed one, but the other bit into her throat. She howled in pain and went down.

Then, the evil ones ran away, leaving eight of their dead behind. But Troy's pack had been badly hurt. John and Miriam were dead, horribly mauled. Tom was lying in human form, moaning, his leg bloody. Troy saw Julia lying in human form, bleeding from her chest, neck, and ear. Troy and the remaining pack members went to human form and rushed to Julia and knelt beside her.

Julia had tears in her eyes. "I'm sorry. I'm so sorry. You and the police weren't supposed to be hurt. Just Troy. He was the only one to be killed."

Troy's eyebrows furrowed. "Me? What are you saying?"

Julia ignored him and looked at the others. "I'm sorry. Please forgive me. That was the agreement." She breathed heavily for a moment. "I fought hard for you. Did you see me? I fought hard for my pack."

Diana leaned close to Julia. "Julia, please tell us what you mean."

"I told the evil pack about your plan. They were supposed to kill Troy, but no one else."

"Why?" Troy asked. "What are you saying? Why did you want me killed?"

She looked at him contemptuously. "You don't know? Hah! Because you humiliated me. You scorned me with that bitch of yours. I wasn't good enough for you, but she was."

Julia grabbed Troy, pulled him close and snarled. "What a slap in the face. So, if I couldn't have you, I'd make sure that she couldn't either. I'd rather you be dead. Well, now she's yours—if you can find her."

"What do you mean, find her?"

Julia started to speak, but stiffened then went limp. Her head fell to the side. Troy took her pulse. He shook his head. "She's dead."

"Did I hear her right?" Hannah asked. "She did this because she was jealous."

"That's what it sounded like," Tom said."

Troy ran a hand through his hair. "I don't know. We'll think about it later. For now, help Tom and load the bodies into our cars. I'm going to check on the cops and try to contact Barb. We'll meet at the cabin later."

* * * * *

His leg bandaged, Tom, with Hannah and Diana, stood in front of three freshly dug graves they for Julia, John and Miriam. They ceremoniously lowered the linen-draped bodies into the graves. They stood there solemnly, despondently. The air had a chill in it and a light breeze ruffled their hair.

They picked up their shovels and filled in the graves, then returned to the cabin and sat in the living room. Hannah and Diana were crying.

Diana shook her head. "I still can't believe what happened. John and Miriam and Julia. All dead. And burying them in that cold, dark forest, without even a grave marker."

Tom put his arm around her. "We've got to be strong, calm ourselves. We've lost pack members before. This will pass. It'll be all right."

Diana wiped her eyes. "Yes, I know. But three at once. That's beyond our experience."

Hannah dropped her head and sobbed. "And Miriam. Poor Miriam. She didn't even have to go. She could have stayed in the hospital. But she wanted to stand with her pack."

Diana put her arm around Hannah. "I know. You two were very close.

They heard a car door slam. "That must be Troy," Tom said. "Thank goodness. It's almost daylight. I was beginning to worry."

Tom opened the door and a bedraggled Troy walked in. He nodded to Tom, then sat with Diana and Hannah. "How's everyone holding up?

"We're hurting," Hanna answered. "But we'll be all right. It'll just take a while."

"Good. You're right. We'll get past this."

Tom turned to Troy. "What happened with the police?"

"Two dead, two wounded, including Sloan. Ambulances were coming when I left."

"What about Barbara?" Hannah asked.

Troy shrugged. "I called her home and her cell three times. No answer. I went to her house. She wasn't there, so I waited until almost daybreak. She didn't show. But her car was there and that worries me. Makes me think she might have been kidnapped."

Tom put his hand on Troy's shoulder. "We'll find her, Troy. We'll scour every inch of this city. We'll find her, my friend."

Hannah and Diana squeezed Troy's hand and nodded in agreement.

"Thanks. But I don't even know if she's alive. Still, I got an idea while I was waiting for her."

Tom's eyes narrowed. "What's that?"

"I don't want to say right now. It might not work. I want to think it through completely."

* * * * *

Troy sat next to Ray on a park bench. "Glad you could make it on such short notice. Thank you."

"It sounded urgent."

"It is. And I need your help. My girlfriend is missing, and I think your pack kidnapped her."

"Why do you think that?"

"I'll explain later. ButI'd bet Thatcher is behind it."

"Thatcher?"

"Yeah. The Police Commissioner. He's your pack leader, right?"

"How did you know?"

"Again, later on. Right now, tell me if you'll help me find her."

Ray stared at Troy. "Why should I? We're friendly at times like this. But we're still mortal enemies."

"Maybe we don't have to be. You and a lot of your pack don't like what you are, right? That's what you told me."

"What's the difference? We can't do anything about it."

"There might be."

"How?"

"By making you a normal person."

"You mean not being a werewolf?"

"Exactly. Barbara—that's her name, my girlfriend. She's a microbiologist and specializes in genetics."

"And?"

"She's working on a cure for Lycanthropy. If she develops it, you and others in your pack are free of your curse. You'd be ordinary human beings."

Ray rubbed his chin. Then, he gave Troy a hard stare. "This better be true, Troy. This is too important, raises expectations too high. If this is a hoax—"

"It's not! I'm telling you, this is for real."

"And you think she can do it?"

"Yes."

Ray dropped his head into his hands, then and looked up with tears in his eyes. "Good god. To be free of this. To be a normal human being. A life without this torture."

"It could happen, Ray. Isn't it worth a chance? What's the downside for you? If it works, you're free. If not, you've lost nothing."

"I've got to think about this."

"There's no time! What if they kill her? Then what? We've got to act now. Right away."

Ray hesitated, then … "Okay, I'll do it."

"Thank you. Do you know where she is?"

"Could be a couple of places. But Thatcher has a condo on the north side. That's probably where he has her."

"Do you know where it is?"

"Yes. I've been there."

"Will you take me there?"

"Yeah. I can do that. We should go now. There's a full moon again tonight. I'm not sure I can control myself. When I transform, I might attack you."

Troy called Tom. "Ray says he might know where Barb is. I'll pick you up in ten minutes."

* * * * *

Troy drove with Tom, following Ray. He looked at his watch. 515 p.m. Troy's head shot forward. "Shit!"

Ahead of them, traffic was backed up. Troy slammed his fist on the steering wheel.

"Dammit!

Troy rubbed his temples. "Tom, go to Ray's car and get Thatcher's address. Get to the condo as fast as possible. Take wolf form if you have to. If you can get Barb out, do it. If not, wait for Ray and me."

Tom jumped out of the car, ran to Ray's then raced off. Troy looked at his watch, then at the sky, which was darkening. Then, he noticed Ray's car managing to maneuver toward the sidewalk. Troy followed. Ray reached the sidewalk and moments later, Troy was behind him. Ray leaned on his horn and drove forward, sending pedestrians scurrying. Troy went right behind him. Once past the bottleneck, they got back on the street and drove to the condo.

As Troy and Ray approached, Tom stepped from behind the building and trotted to them. "Barb is okay. But she's got two cops and the Police Commissioner with her."

"We've got to move fast," Ray said. "The sun is going down soon. I'll knock on the door, and when it's opened we rush in and get your girlfriend."

* * * * *

Troy and Tom were in wolf form to the side of Ray, out of sight from the doorway. Ray knocked on the door. Thatcher opened it. He looked suspiciously at Ray. "What are you doing here? You're supposed to be—"

Thatcher pulled a snub-nosed revolver from his shoulder holster and, as Troy and Tom rushed in, pointed it at Barbara.

"One move," Thatcher said. "Just twitch and she's a memory."

They stopped.

"Take human form."

Troy and Tom obey.

"Damn! I wish I could do that whenever I wanted."

Barbara's face was flushed. Thatcher closed the door and looked at Troy. "What a bonus. The pack leader, right? " He looked at Barbara. "See, I said you'd come in handy."

He told the policemen to cuff Troy and Tom. They do, then push them onto a couch. Thatcher looked at Ray. "And you, you son of a bitch, what are you up to? Betraying your own kind? Turn around and face the wall."

Ray did and Thatcher clubbed him on the head with the butt of his pistol. Ray fell, semiconscious.

Troy gave Thatcher a hard stare. "What's with you? We only protect people and fight your pack in self-defense. What's your bitch with us?"

"Lots of things," he said smiling. "But one is that you're giving werewolves a good name."

"Very funny." Troy gestured with his head toward Barbara. "At least let her go. She's not one of us."

Thatcher looked at his watch and out the window as the sun began to set.

"We'll talk about it tomorrow."

One of the policemen shuddered and began the agonizing transformation to wolf form, then the other, and finally, Thatcher.

Ray, still on the floor, transformed and struggled to all fours. Barbara began to scream, but one of the wolves put its teeth on her throat.

Ray trembled. He shook his head and scrapped his paws on the floor. He growled, bared his teeth and looked at Troy and Tom, and finally at Barbara.

He leapt at the wolf with its teeth on Barbara's neck.

Troy and Tom took wolf form and broke out of their cuffs.

Tom attacked one wolf, but Troy noticed Thatcher backing away toward the window. Troy leapt at him, but Thatcher fought him ferociously, forcing him back. Troy attacked again, but Thatcher drove him back and off his feet momentarily. Then he spun around and jumped through the window, shattering the glass.

Troy hurdled through the window after Thatcher and landed next to him. The two squared off. They grappled, then Thatcher tried to run away, but Troy followed and jumped on Thatcher's back. Thatcher tried to shake him off, but Troy hung on and bit deeply into the back of his opponent's neck. Thatcher wailed, staggered back and fell, dead. He went to human form.

Troy dragged him into the bushes, then jumped back through the broken window and changed into human form.

The two evil werewolves were in human form, dead. Tom was in human form. Ray, still in wolf form, was wounded in the shoulder. He lied motionless on his side, panting heavily and occasionally whimpered.

Troy rushed to Barbara.

"How are you?"

"I don't know. I mean, I think I'm okay."

Troy squeezed her hand and kissed her cheek. "You'll be all right. I'll make sure of it."

* * * * *

Ray had transformed to human form at daylight and now sat with the other pack members in the sun-filled room living room of the cabin. Troy was bandaged on his neck and arm. Ray's shirt was off, and Hannah was working his shoulder. She finished and tapped him on the back.

"Okay. All done."

"It feels better already. You do good work." He looked at the others. "All of you are lucky to have her."

"Thanks. And you're welcome."

"Think I'll need a rabies shot?"

Hannah smiled. "I doubt it."

Troy turned to Ray. "Thanks again for what you did."

"It was tough. Everything inside me was screaming to kill you. Doesn't matter. I'm glad I did it."

"So are we."

"I feel good," Ray said. "Like I haven't in a long time."

"Happy to hear it," Troy said. "So, what happens now that your leader is dead?"

"They'll find another pretty quickly. And they'll be out again next full moon."

Ray turned to Barbara. "Can we talk about the cure?"

"I'm close, but it'll be a while."

"How long?"

"Four, maybe five weeks."

"What? In a month there'll be another full moon and—"

Troy held up his hands. "I've been thinking about that. Would you stay with us during the full moon? We'd have to tie you down."

"That's okay. I've got to do it. I don't want to kill anyone else."

Troy grinned. "Tom and Hannah will stay with

you. I'm sure Hannah will find a strong sedative. That may help."

"I hope so. But if I give you any trouble, kick my ass."

"I can get me some Versed. That's a powerful tranquilizer."

Ray looked at Barbara." Hurry up with that serum, will you?"

"I will. I promise."

* * * * *

A month later, Ray sat with Troy and his pack.

"How you feeling?" Troy asked Ray.

"All right, I guess. But I'm nervous."

Tom turned to Ray. "Who wouldn't be?"

Hannah holds up a liquid-filled clear plastic bag. "Versed. A heavy dose. Three milliliters. That'll put you in la-la land. You'll get it intravenously through-out the night."

Troy added. "But we'll still have to chain you down anyway."

"That's okay. I suppose I'll be fit to be tied."
They laughed.

Troy peeked outside as a bright full moon lightens the darkening sky. "I think it's time."

Ray nodded. "Yeah. Let's get it done."

"All right. Go with Tom and Hannah. Diana and I have to go on patrol."

"Fine. Listen, thank you all. I'm glad I met you." Diana moved to Ray and kissed him on the cheek. "So are we. Good luck."

* * * * *

Ray was in the finished basement of the cabin. He was in wolf form and chained to a bed and sleeping with an intravenous needle in his arm that's attached to the Versed. Tom and Hannah were playing cards at a nearby table. Hannah glanced at her watch. 4:30 a.m.

Ray began to fidget, then started to shudder and tried to break out of the chains. His eyes opened and he growled fiercely. Tom and Hannah rushed to him. Hannah checked the intravenous connection and tapped the plastic bag. Tom leaned over Ray.

"Ray! Ray, can you hear me?"

Ray howled, his head snapped from side to side, struggling with the chains. Hannah and Tom tried to hold him down, but Ray got one paw loose and swiped at Tom, slashing his cheek. Tom jumped back.

Tom shouted, "Go to wolf form! We can't hold him like this."

In the moments before they took wolf form, Ray broke free, jumped from the bed, leapt at Tom, and bit him in the paw. Hannah jumped on Ray and tried to pull him down. But Ray fought her off. Tom moved in, snapping at Ray as Hannah again tried to take him down. Ray sprung at Tom and bit him in the shoulder.

The fight continued and finally Tom bit into Ray's neck. Hannah went for his chest. Ray writhed, then stiffened. He fell, and went limp, breathing heavily. His eyes showed sadness. He whimpered and put a paw gently on Hannah's. His breathing slowed. A tear rolled down his snout. He exhaled deeply and his head fell to the side. He went to human form. So did Tom and Hannah. Tom's face had a gash in it and his shoulder and foot were bleeding. Hannah was unscathed. She reached for Ray's pulse.

"He's dead. Dammit! A few hours more and he'd have made it."

"We did our best not to kill him. He just wouldn't stop fighting. We had no choice. He might have killed one of us."

* * * * *

Troy and the pack were in the living room. "He still downstairs?" Troy asked.

"Yeah," Tom said. "We wrapped him in linen. "We'll bury him when it gets dark. I'm sorry this happened, but there was nothing else you could do."

"So, what do we do now?" Diana asked. "Ray was supposed to help us get the serum to the other wolves."

"We'll have to go out the next full moon and somehow offer it to them."

* * * * *

A full moon glowed as the pack prepared to go on patrol.

"Okay," Troy said. "When we run into some evil ones, show no aggression. I'll take human form and approach them. You all stay close in case they attack."

"I don't think you should go to human form," Diana said. "That's dangerous."

"I don't want anything to go wrong. When they see me go human, they'll know I'm not planning any violence."

"Okay. You're the leader. But I don't like it."

* * * * *

The pack prowled through a nearby park. Troy's nose twitched, and he and the rest of the pack turned to their right, where nine wolves are moving toward them. As they near, Troy takes human form and approaches them.

"I am not here as an enemy. I am here as a friend. Please hear me out."

The wolves look at each other. None move.

"I know many of you hate what you are and what you do."

Some of the wolves nodded their heads.

"There is a way out for you. We have a serum that can change you into normal human beings."

Five of the wolves moved forward, their tails and heads lowered. The four other wolves growled at them. But the five bared their teeth and growled back. The four attacked them and a vicious fight ensued. Troy stepped back and his pack moved closer to him. Troy held up his hand and looked over his shoulder.

"Don't come any closer. They've attacked the ones who want the serum. But I can't tell which is which."

The fight continued. Three wolves are killed. Finally, two of them run away. Four others moved slowly to Troy.

"You want the serum?"

They nodded.

"Okay. Be on the east side of the Pritzker Building of Millennium Park tomorrow morning at ten."

The wolves nodded and walked away.

* * * * *

Troy and his pack, in human form, sat on benches waiting. Two men approached them. One of them asked. "Are you the ones we met last night? The ones with the serum?"

"Yes, we are." Troy said. He held out his hand and the man gripped it.

"My name is Ben Hauser. Pleased to meet you."

"Likewise. I'm Troy Wellstone."

Ben turned to the other man. "This is Tom Bishop."

Troy shook his hand, then introduced his pack.

Shortly, four more men and two women approached. One of the men said, "We're here for the serum."

* * * * *

Troy was with Barbara sitting in her living room. She gave him a kiss on the cheek. "That went well."

"Yes, it did. We'll have to check on them the next full moon. But if you say it'll work, it'll work. And there'll be a lot fewer evil ones."

Troy slouched further into the couch, a hint of a smile on his face. Barbara sidled close to him, and he put his arm around her.

"You seem about as content as I've ever seen you," Barbara said.

"I am. We've done a lot of good. You saved those people from a horrible fate. Ordinary folks are safer. Plus, the best woman in the world is in love with me. How could I not be content?"

"Troy."

"What?"

"Marry me."

"Ah, you're a forward wench."

"Yep. When it comes to us, I get right to the point."

"Come on, Barb. I'm a werewolf."

"Eh. Nobody's perfect."

"What about the chance that we'd have—"

"A baby?"

"Yeah."

"With all the precautions you take? Besides, we might not have to worry about that."

"What do you mean?"

Barbara gave him a coy smile.

"I'm a scientist, Troy. Let's just say I'm working on something."

Troy grinned. "I can't wait to find out what it is."

Frank Victoria

Frank graduated with a journalism degree from Northern Illinois University and used his skills to make words his livelihood. He was a professional editor and writer for a variety of trade magazines with an expertise in the petroleum marketing industry.

Picking up a book by an author he followed, the idea for *The Founders' Plot* gushered like a new oil well bursting through the earth.

Most writers know that once words are part of their DNA, they never leave. His next step was to add teacher to his resume where for 16 years, he taught in the Chicago Public School System with an emphasis on history and civics.

A proud Marine Corps veteran, Frank calls Chicago home and enjoys the glory of the Magnificent Mile and Lakeshore Drive running along Lake Michigan. If you meet Frank, ask him about Maxwell Street and the mouth-watering polish sausage and pork chop sandwiches covered with grilled onions!

How to Work
with Frank Victoria

Frank Victoria is also the award-winning author
of *The Founders' Plot.*

Based in the Chicago area, Frank would be delighted
to work virtually with Book Clubs via Zoom
to discuss *The Founders' Plot.*

Within the book are several Discussion Questions
to begin a session … or your club members
may have their own list.

To schedule a date and time, Contact Frank at:
708-218-3144
FVquiller@gmail.com
FrankVictoriaAuthor.com

@FrankVAuthor

@FrankVictoriaAuthor

bit.ly/FrankVLinkedin

https://www.facebook.com/AuthorFrankVictoria
@AuthorFrankVictoria

Other Novellas
by Frank Victoria

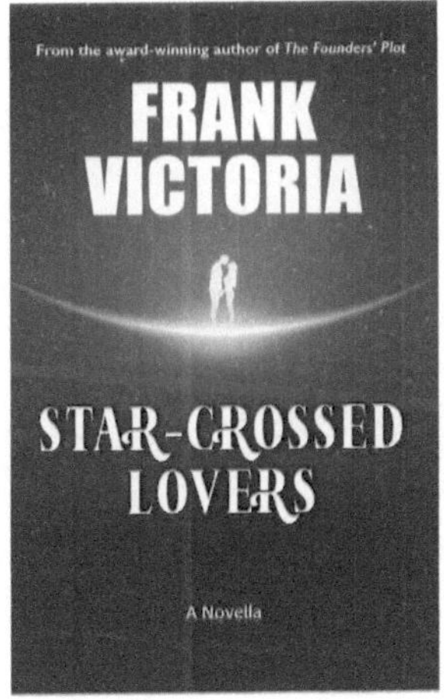

www.ingramcontent.com/pod-product-compliance
Lightning Source LLC
Chambersburg PA
CBHW022022150726
47990CB00002B/775